D1639574

re &

DUNDEE

Pass the Parcel

DUNDEE CITY COUNCIL

LOCATION
CENTRAL CHILDREN'S

ACCESSION NUMBER
C01 099 043X

SUPPLIER | PRICE
ASKEWS | £9.99

CLASS No. | DATE
2·6·23

by **Sarah Snashall** and **Lucy Makuc**

FRANKLIN WATTS
LONDON•SYDNEY

Dad put the music on.

"Pass the parcel, Bel,"
he said.

3

"Stop! Open it!" Dad said.

Dad put the music on.

"Pass the parcel," he said.

"Stop! Open it!" Dad said.

Dad put the music on.

"Pass the parcel," he said.

"Stop! Open it!" Dad said.

Dad put the music on.

"Pass the parcel," he said.

15

"Stop! Open it, Bel,"
Dad said.

"Happy birthday, Bel,"
Dad said.

19

Story trail

Start at the beginning of the story trail. Ask your child to retell the story in their own words, pointing to each picture in turn to recall the sequence of events.

Start

Independent Reading

This series is designed to provide an opportunity for your child to read on their own. These notes are written for you to help your child choose a book and to read it independently.

In school, your child's teacher will often be using reading books which have been banded to support the process of learning to read. Use the book band colour your child is reading in school to help you make a good choice. *Pass the Parcel* is a good choice for children reading at Red Band in their classroom to read independently.

The aim of independent reading is to read this book with ease, so that your child enjoys the story and relates it to their own experiences.

About the book
It's Bel's birthday, and she is playing Pass the Parcel with her friends. The parcel is passed from person to person, but who will win the prize inside it?

Before reading
Help your child to learn how to make good choices by asking: "Why did you choose this book? Why do you think you will enjoy it?" Support your child to think about what they already know about the story context. Look at the cover together and ask: "What do you think the story will be about?" Read the title aloud and ask: "What do you think Pass the Parcel is?"

Remind your child that they can try to sound out the letters to make a word if they get stuck.

Decide together whether your child will read the story independently or read it aloud to you. When books are short, as at Red Band, your child may wish to do both!

During reading

If reading aloud, support your child if they hesitate or ask for help by telling them the word. Remind your child of what they know and what they can do independently.

If reading to themselves, remind your child that they can come and ask for your help if stuck.

After reading

Support comprehension by asking your child to tell you about the story. Use the story trail to encourage your child to retell the story in the right sequence, in their own words.

Give your child a chance to respond to the story: "Did you have a favourite part? Have you ever played Pass the Parcel at a party?" Help your child think about the messages in the book that go beyond the story and ask: "Why does Bel have to win the game?" "What is the prize inside the parcel?"

Extending learning

Help your child extend the story structure by using the same sentence pattern and adding some more elements. For example, playing a game of Musical Statues. Dad put the music on. Everybody danced. Dad stopped the music. "Stop!" said Dad. Bel moved.

On a few of the pages, check your child can finger point accurately by asking them to show you how they kept their place in the print by tracking from word to word.

Help your child to use letter information by asking them to find the interest word on each page by using the first letter. For example: "Which word is 'parcel'? How do you know it is that word?"

Franklin Watts
First published in Great Britain in 2023
by Hodder & Stoughton

Copyright © Hodder & Stoughton Limited, 2023

All rights reserved.

Series Editors: Jackie Hamley and Melanie Palmer
Series Advisors and Development Editors: Dr Sue Bodman and Glen Franklin
Series Designers: Cathryn Gilbert and Peter Scoulding

A CIP catalogue record for this book is
available from the British Library.

ISBN 978 1 4451 7670 3 (hbk)
ISBN 978 1 4451 7669 7 (pbk)
ISBN 978 1 4451 8822 5 (ebook)

Printed in China

Franklin Watts
An imprint of
Hachette Children's Group
Part of Hodder & Stoughton
Carmelite House
50 Victoria Embankment
London EC4Y 0DZ

An Hachette UK Company
www.hachette.co.uk

www.reading-champion.co.uk

FSC
www.fsc.org
MIX
Paper from
responsible sources
FSC® C104740